FOR DICK SCHENA

BEWARE
OF
DOG

Clarion Books
Ticknor & Fields, a Houghton Mifflin Company

Copyright © 1983 by Dick Gackenbach

Library of Congress Cataloging in Publication Data
Gackenbach, Dick.   Binky gets a car.
Summary: When Binky get his first fast-pedaling car, he ignores the rules of the road and
learns painfully that to be a driver, one must watch where he is going.
[1. Automobile driving—Fiction]   I. Title.
PZ7. G117Bi   1983   [E]   82-9593   ISBN 0-89919-144-4

Y 10 9 8 7 6 5 4 3 2 1

Binky Gets a Car

by Dick Gackenbach

CLARION BOOKS

Ticknor & Fields: A Houghton Mifflin Company

NEW YORK

Binky McNab
got his first car
for his birthday.
It was bright red and shiny.
It was chrome-plated.
It had two honking horns.
And it had the finest two pedals
that money could buy!

"Drive carefully, son,"
said Binky's father.

"Watch where you're going, dear!" said his mother.

"VAR-ROOM-M-M!"

said Binky McNab.

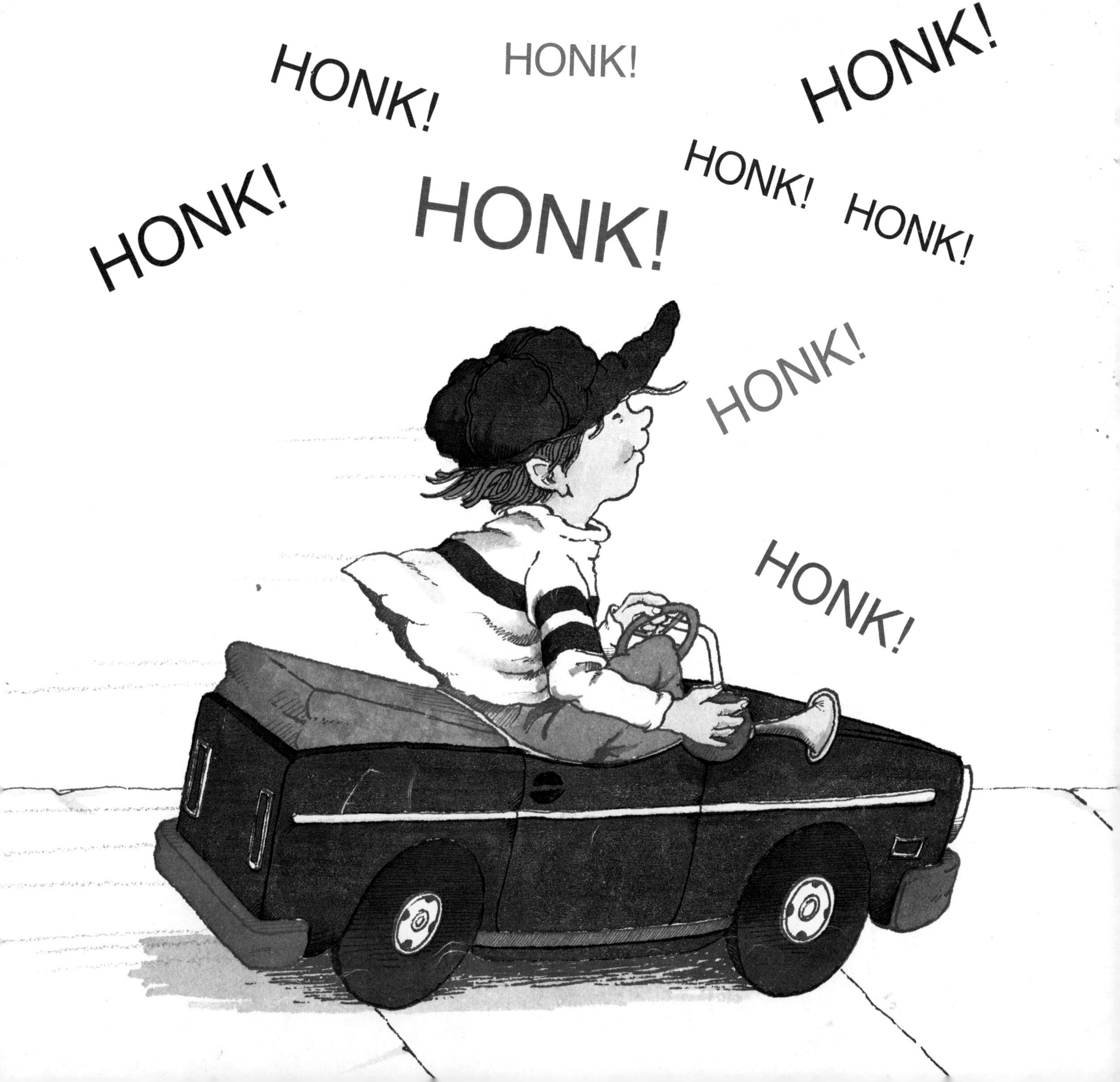
HONK!
HONK!
HONK!
HONK!
HONK!
HONK!
HONK!
HONK!
HONK!

"That's him! That's the one!" everyone said.
"Uh-oh!" said Binky.

Binky's mother took his honking horns away.
Binky's father said,
"You'll have to stay inside our yard
until you learn to drive with care."

"Look how well Binky is
driving now," said his father.
"I hope you're right,"
said his mother.

"AGH-H-H-H!" his father screamed.

"Oh dear!" his mother cried.

"Oops," said Binky McNab.